BL 4.5

W9-ALN-154

NIKKI & DEJA

WEDDING DRAMA

by Karen English

Illustrated by Laura Freeman

Clarion Books
Houghton Mifflin Harcourt
Boston ★ New York
2012

To all the Nikkis and Dejas everywhere
—K.E.

For Roberta
—L.F.

Clarion Books
215 Park Avenue South
New York, New York 10003

Text copyright © 2012 by Karen English
Illustrations copyright © 2012 by Laura Freeman

Clarion Books is an imprint of Houghton Mifflin Harcourt Publishing Company.

www.hmhbooks.com

The text of this book was set in 13.5 Warnock Pro.
The illustrations were executed digitally.

Library of Congress Cataloging-in-Publication Data
English, Karen.
Nikki & Deja : wedding drama / by Karen English ; illustrated by Laura Freeman.
p. cm.
Summary: Ms. Shelby's third-grade girls are so excited about her upcoming wedding
that they start a wedding planning competition, which drives a wedge between best
friends Nikki and Deja, the two whose names were drawn to attend the event.
ISBN 978-0-547-61564-6
[1. Weddings—Fiction. 2. Teachers—Fiction. 3. Schools—Fiction. 4. Best friends—Fiction.
5. Friendship—Fiction. 6. African Americans—Fiction.] I. Freeman-Hines, Laura, ill. II. Title.
III. Title: Nikki and Deja, wedding drama. IV. Title: Wedding drama.
PZ7.E7232Njo 2012
[Fic]—dc23
2011027484

Manufactured in the United States of America
DOC 10 9 8 7 6 5 4 3 2 1
4500342966

– Contents –

Fair and Square

Deja

There is something strange going on. Something in the air. Deja feels it as soon as she enters Room Ten at Carver Elementary School. She looks over at her best friend, Nikki, to see if she's feeling it, too, but Nikki is busy pulling her homework out of her folder to drop it in the basket on Ms. Shelby's desk. Deja looks at the other kids. They're doing their usual first-thing-in-the-morning stuff. Gavin, the new boy, is sitting in his chair with his hands folded. Carlos is taking tiny action figures out of his backpack and squirreling them away in his desk. Antonia and Casey are whispering back and forth—probably backbiting. Nikki says *backbiting* is her mom's new word. It means something like gossip, which people shouldn't do. So now Nikki is all the time reminding Deja that if you can't say anything nice about someone, you shouldn't say anything at all. Deja personally thinks she'd have to be some kind of perfect person to say only nice things all the time. How could someone be lunch monitor if he or she could report only on the good stuff the kids at their lunch table did? How could a monitor report on someone talking with a mouth full of food? She'd said that to Nikki, and Nikki had to agree.

Suddenly, Deja knows what it is that's strange. It's Ms. Shelby. She's just standing there at the front of the class with a secret smile on her lips as she watches the kids go through their morning routines. She isn't doing anything else. She isn't doing any of her usual fussing. She isn't marking things in her scary book—the one with all their scores and grades and stuff. She's just standing there looking at the class with this funny smile on her face. Deja looks over at Nikki. She's pulled out the entire contents of her desk, and now she's going through a bunch of balled-up papers that had been crammed in at the back. Nikki is such a neatnik.

Deja hurries over to her and says, "You know Ms. Shelby doesn't like it when we pull everything out of our desks without permission."

Nikki frowns. "It's not going to take me long." She goes off to get the classroom trash can. She places it beside her desk so she can sweep out the pencil shavings that have accumulated inside it.

Deja glances over at Ms. Shelby. Now she has her hands clasped behind her back. She's still smiling as she stands there gazing at her class as if her mind is someplace else.

It's almost like the time when Ms. Shelby got her engagement ring and she waited until all her students had settled down before showing it off. Today, it seems that everyone has slowed their morning routine as if they have all the time in the world. Only Gavin, the new boy, and a few others are ready and waiting. Deja returns to her desk and looks at the whiteboard. There's no journal topic posted. What's going on? She takes out her morning journal, places it in the exact middle of her desk, and then folds her hands.

Finally, Ms. Shelby speaks. "I love the way Row Four is ready and waiting." She moves to the board and puts a tally mark beside Row Four's space. Deja looks at her classmates two rows over. It's true. They are all in their seats, ready and waiting. How did that happen? She doesn't like when Ms. Shelby catches them off guard like that. Row Four has seven points from the day before. Row Two, where Deja sits, has three measly points. She glares at Carlos's back. He's the weak link. Ms. Shelby has told them about how a chain is only as strong as its weakest link—which doesn't seem all that fair to Deja. Carlos with his outbursts and rule-breaking is the weak link of Row Two. It's not fair.

Ms. Shelby turns back to the students. Her smile is even wider now. "Okay, class," she says. "I have a wonderful announcement." She looks around, as if measuring how her students are taking this bit of information. Everyone quiets. Those who were still milling about now take their seats. Deja hopes it's not another school election. That was Ms. Shelby's big news a few months before. Deja ran for student body president of Carver Elementary School and lost, and she's still trying to get over it. She is pondering this when she hears Ms. Shelby say, "You know, I'm getting married in less than two weeks." All the girls look around at one another and smile. The boys look blank, as if they're thinking, *So?* Deja bets they're probably still hoping for a pizza party.

Deja glances at Nikki. She's just sitting there with her mouth partially open, looking as if she's listening very carefully.

Ms. Shelby continues, "I so wished all of you

could come to my wedding, but that's not possible. There just isn't room." Now the girls look deflated. The boys don't seem to be bothered. The new boy, Gavin, has a tiny frown on his face, as if he's just trying to understand what's going on. Deja wonders about him for a moment. So far he's been quiet, but there's something about him that doesn't seem all that quiet. It's like he's trying super hard to be good because maybe he wasn't so good at his old school.

Ms. Shelby goes on. "But it just wouldn't feel right if I had *no one* from my class there." She pauses again. *For effect,* Deja thinks. Ms. Shelby loves to see who's hanging on her every word. The girls are, of course. Nikki's mouth has dropped open even further, in anticipation.

"But yesterday I discovered that four of my guests can't come. That means I have room for four people. Two of *you,* plus a parent or guardian."

Now there are happy gasps from every girl.

"Since I can only invite two of you, I think the best way to be fair is to have a drawing."

Now some of the girls look around at each other suspiciously. Who's going to pick the lucky "tickets"?

Ralph raises his hand. "Ms. Shelby," he says

before he has waited to be recognized. "What if two girls win?"

"Win?"

"The tickets," he says.

Ms. Shelby, still in her good mood, laughs. "No matter, Ralph. It will still be fair because everyone has an *equal* chance."

The word *equal* makes Deja think of math, which is not her best subject. She looks over at the star beside Nikki's name on the Facts Quiz chart. Nikki is almost caught up to Erik. He's on his eights and she just passed the sixes on the last multiplication facts quiz. Nikki told Deja she likes that Ms. Shelby uses big fat stars, so that they can be seen from everywhere in the room. Her star is red, the happiest color of all, Nikki says. Deja, unfortunately, seems to be stuck on her fives, which is almost as easy as the twos or ones. She wonders if she will ever master anything beyond that. When she turns her attention back to the front of the room, she sees that Ms. Shelby is holding a stack of index cards that have been cut in half.

"I want you to put your names on these cards. Then you're going to drop them in this box." She holds up an old tissue box that has the top cut off. "I'm going to give it a big shake and draw out two names. And then . . ." Her voice trails off. "How many think that's fair?"

All the students' hands eventually go up. Some a little reluctantly, it seems.

"I wish I could have you all there, but . . ." Ms. Shelby's voice trails off again, and she shrugs and places the index cards on ChiChi's desk.

ChiChi is the paper monitor for the week. She jumps up and says in a slightly whiny voice, "Can I have a helper?" She glances quickly at Keisha.

"Sure," Ms. Shelby says.

When all the students have written their names on their cards, ChiChi and Keisha go around and collect them and then put them in the special box on Ms. Shelby's desk. Deja has embellished her name card with daisies and balloons, thinking perhaps it might give her some good luck.

Ms. Shelby picks up the box and gives it a shake, making a point of not looking in it. She reaches in and gives the cards a little stir. Deja holds her breath. She looks over at Nikki and can tell she's holding hers as well. Ms. Shelby reaches in and pulls out a card.

Deja recognizes it immediately. It's hers! The balloons and daisies are clearly visible. Ms. Shelby has pulled her card!

"Deja!" Ms. Shelby says, full of enthusiasm.

Nearly all the girls in the class turn to her in unison. A few have suspicious looks on their faces. Deja claps her hand over her mouth, her eyes wide. She looks at Nikki again. Nikki's lips are parted with surprise and she seems frozen in place. Deja can't tell what she is feeling. Then Nikki turns to Deja and gives her a weak smile. Oh, no. Deja hopes that she isn't . . . *jealous.*

Ms. Shelby is smiling at her, and Deja feels that something is expected.

"Thank you, Ms. Shelby," she says quietly, as if, by saying it quietly, those who were hoping their name would be called might not realize that their chances have just been cut in half.

"Okay," Ms. Shelby says, once again stirring the cards in the box slowly, mixing everything up to show her fairness. "One more invite to go."

Deja is hoping that it isn't a boy. If it is, the teasing will start right away, probably led by Ralph or Carlos: *Ooh, Deja and whoever, sitting in a tree, k-i-s-s-i*—Deja can't even bring herself to finish spelling out the word. She closes her eyes and holds her breath.

Then a miracle happens—something so startling, she can't believe she heard Ms. Shelby correctly. Did she say *Nikki?* Did she really say Nikki's

name? She must have, because immediately a chorus of moans and groans and "That's not *fair!*" starts up, until Ms. Shelby has to raise her hand and put the forefinger of the other hand over her lips. She has to look around in that fashion until everyone has settled down.

When the class is finally quiet, several girls—especially Keisha and ChiChi—show their displeasure with furrowed brows, poked-out lips, and sucking of the teeth as loudly as they can muster. Antonia has the ability to raise one eyebrow, and she does this now and holds it while moving her pursed lips to one side. Though she is looking down, anyone can tell that she heartily disapproves. Then she turns and whispers something to her best friend, Casey, who sits behind her.

All of this just encourages Ms. Shelby to deliver—in not too many words, thankfully—one of her standard speeches about fairness and accepting results, even if you don't like them, when things are *fair and square,* and a bunch of other stuff. Deja doesn't really pay attention because she's just fine with the results. In fact, she's so fine she's afraid to look over at Nikki. They both might just break out into huge smiles.

"We're going to Ms. Shelby's wedding," Deja says as they walk slowly toward the handball court. "We're going to Ms. Shelby's wedding!"

"I can't believe it," Nikki adds. She takes out one of the invitations Ms. Shelby gave her and Deja after she dismissed the class for morning recess. Ms. Shelby had held them back until all the other kids had gone.

"I didn't want to give you these in front of your classmates," she'd said. "That would have made them feel worse."

The invitations are beautiful. Deja takes hers out as well, and stares at it. "It was fair and square," she repeats after a minute or so, as if she has to convince herself.

"Yeah, it was fair and square."

That's not exactly how Keisha sees it from her place in line behind Deja when recess is over. "I don't think people who are best friends should get to go," she says in a whisper at Deja's neck.

"Ms. Shelby says it was fair and square, and I go by what Ms. Shelby says," Deja replies over her shoulder.

Keisha ignores this. Obviously, she has a

solution. "One of you should let someone else go in your place."

"No," Deja says immediately. "One of us is not going to do that. We're both going."

"Not fair," Keisha says under her breath in a hissing sound.

Deja shrugs, but she feels a little funny.

Happily, as the day goes on, acceptance that it will be Nikki and Deja going to the wedding seems to grow, and attention shifts to Ms. Shelby's wedding dress. It's Rosario's idea to imagine what the dress will look like. And the idea seems to take hold. During the rest of the morning, at every possible opportunity, the girls work on drawings of Ms. Shelby's wedding dress—what they would like to see their teacher wear, if they had their way.

All day they pull out the drawings to touch them up: after spelling activities, after math workshop, during free time. Finally, at lunch recess, all the girls bring their artwork to Room Ten's outside table to scrutinize one another's creations.

Nikki unfolds hers carefully and holds it down. A circle of heads gather over it. There's silence for a moment, and then Ayanna says thoughtfully, "I like the colors. Kind of." Nikki has drawn Ms. Shelby in a long yellow and blue gown that's clingy on top but then billows out in a big fluffy circle.

"But it's not white," ChiChi says. "Wedding dresses have to be white."

"They don't have to be," Nikki says quickly. "You can have any color you want."

Next, Deja puts hers down for all to see. She has drawn Ms. Shelby's dress in lavender and made a train for the dress that swirls down and around and all over the paper. It's quite different, and several girls *ooh* and *ahh* as if they wish they had thought to make a wedding dress train that swirled all over the paper.

Keisha has the best drawing. She has pictured Ms. Shelby in a long white dress with a fluffy white shawl. Plus, she's drawn a tiara, making their teacher look just like a princess. Keisha is the best artist in the class.

When everyone looks up, Yolanda says, "I wonder what everybody's going to eat at Ms. Shelby's wedding." Deja can tell that Yolanda's mouth is watering at the thought of it. "I wonder what kind of wedding cake she's going to have," Yolanda continues. Her eyes drift up to the sky as she's imagining it. "Let's draw wedding cakes!" she says suddenly.

They all sit back down at the outdoor table, turn their papers over to the clean side, and begin to create elaborate wedding cakes. Ayanna makes hers fifteen-tiered, with alternating pink and blue icing.

"That looks more like a baby shower cake," Keisha says, eyeing Ayanna's drawing. ChiChi's eyes get big, then everyone bursts into giggles.

"It does not!" Ayanna protests. "Baby shower cakes don't come in tiers!"

"What are tiers?" Yolanda asks.

"These things," Ayanna says, pointing to the layers on her drawing.

The freeze bell rings then, and everyone sits perfectly still until the second bell signals that it's time to line up. Each girl carries her drawing carefully to her place in Room Ten's lineup spot.

With My Own Two Eyes
Nikki

A funny thing happens later that day. It happens when Nikki goes to the office to deliver the book fair money. It's her turn to be office monitor, which is really the best thing to be. There's always something that has to go to the office—or something that has to be retrieved from the office. It's the most wonderful thing to hear Ms. Shelby say, "I need the office monitor to take ___ to the office." Excitement flutters in Nikki's stomach as she rises from her seat—to the envy of the rest of the class—and walks in a very officious way to Ms. Shelby's desk. She has a grand sense of importance as she walks down the hall and feels the eyes of some of the other kids on her when she passes their open classroom doors. It's hard to keep from smiling. She has this special permission that they don't have. She loves hearing Mrs. Marker, the office lady, say, "Thank you, Nikki," as she solemnly hands over the important folder. It's reassuring that someone in the office knows her name. She's the *office monitor.* There are only a few other kids at Carver Elementary who can make that claim.

This afternoon when Nikki opens the door to the office she sees a big bouquet of roses sitting on the counter, the one where all the important handouts for parents are stacked. The one with the pencil on a string and the list of volunteer hours where parents put check marks; the one with a small bell that visitors can ring when everyone behind the counter is too busy to notice that they are standing there waiting. Today, standing beside the big vase of roses, a man is waiting patiently. He is not very tall and he's wearing glasses. He looks like a man who might have been super smart when he was a little boy. He waits, and Nikki waits. No one is on the other side of the counter. She wishes he would just ring the bell, and she wonders why he doesn't. She can't ring the bell because she is just a kid. So she has to wait.

After a minute that feels like an hour, Mrs. Marker returns to the counter. She doesn't see

Nikki standing there with the folder. She just sees the man with the flowers. She gives him a big smile.

"I bet I know who those are for," she says.

"I bet you do, too," the man says in a quiet voice.

Nikki's ears perk up.

"Well, you know she's in class now, but I can make sure she gets them at afternoon recess."

"That'll be great," the man says. He has a really shy smile, Nikki sees. And his voice is so quiet. She wonders who those roses could be for. They're probably for a teacher, because it's not graduation day, when parents bring bunches of balloons and flowers for their graduates. But they could be for someone's birthday. A girl . . . The man must be somebody's daddy. Boy, is she ever lucky.

"Nikki, are you deaf?"

Mrs. Marker is reaching her hand out for the folder.

"Oh!" Nikki says, startled.

The man smiles down at her then, and Nikki feels even more startled, and a little bit embarrassed. She hands over the folder and turns toward the door.

"Wait a sec, Nikki," Mrs. Marker says. "Could

you tell your teacher that there's something really special in the office for her?" Mrs. Marker winks at the man. He smiles shyly again.

"Don't forget. Tell her it's something from someone she knows."

The man smiles at Nikki now. She can feel that smile as she goes out the door and all the way down the hall. She knows who he is. She is sure. That man is Ms. Shelby's fiancé. That short, soft-spoken man is Ms. Shelby's *fiancé!* Wait until she tells Deja! Wait until she tells all the other girls! She, Nikki, alone, has seen with her own two eyes *Ms. Shelby's fiancé.*

As soon as she enters Room Ten, she delivers the message as promised, then watches Ms. Shelby's face closely. "Thank you, Nikki," is all she says. The class is quiet with a workbook assignment, and Ms. Shelby is busy with her grade book. Nikki looks at the stack of spelling tests on Ms. Shelby's desk and glances quickly at the test she'd been correcting. Nikki almost laughs when she sees all the red marks on Ralph's paper. He never bothers to study, even though Ms. Shelby gives them a pretest the day before the real test. And on the day of the real test, Ms. Shelby tells the class she's rooting for them. Nikki thinks that when your teacher is rooting for you, you should at least try.

As she heads for her desk, she looks over at Deja and makes her eyes real big. Deja looks puzzled. It is their signal that one of them knows something really important that the other one doesn't know.

"What?" Deja mouths.

In answer, Nikki purses her lips as if she's whistling and looks up at the ceiling.

Deja frowns. She doesn't like to be in the dark.

As soon as Ms. Shelby lets them out for afternoon recess, Deja grabs Nikki's arm and says, "What's going on?"

"I saw Ms. Shelby's fiancé."

Rosario, walking practically on Nikki's heels, exclaims, "Ms. Shelby's fiancé?"

Nikki whips around. "Yes. I saw him *with my own two eyes.*" She feels a little bit powerful stating this.

"What's he look like?" Deja asks.

Antonia gets wind of this and sidles over. She doesn't say anything. She just stands there as a small crowd gathers around Nikki and Deja and Rosario. They're all waiting to hear what their teacher's fiancé looks like.

"My auntie has a fiancé," Yolanda states proudly. "She has a ring and everything." She only gets a moment of attention from the group of girls. They have more important things to find out, it seems.

"Tell us everything," Ayanna says.

"Well, he's kinda short."

Rosario's shoulders sink with disappointment.

"And he wears glasses."

"Glasses," Yolanda says in a low voice, as if the thought of Ms. Shelby's fiancé wearing glasses is too strange to comprehend.

"And I think he speaks another language along with American."

"Another language," Deja says. "Like what?"

"I think Spanish."

"My mom and dad speak Spanish," Rosario says. "And my grandparents and my two aunts and all of my uncles, and I can, too, if I want to."

"I never heard you speak Spanish," Ayanna says. "Say something in Spanish."

"Buenos días," Rosario says.

"Anybody can say *buenos días,*" Antonia— who almost never says anything because she mainly likes to listen—declares.

Everyone turns to her in surprise.

"Yeah," Yolanda agrees. "Everyone knows *buenos días.*"

✻

"What else does he look like?" Deja asks as they're walking home from school.

Nikki sighs. Deja's already asked that, but Nikki doesn't have anything more to add. "He just looks ordinary."

Deja frowns. Nikki knows she is wondering how their beloved Ms. Shelby can have a fiancé who just looks ordinary.

"What was he wearing?" Deja asks.

"Pants and a shirt and a jacket."

"How did he act?"

"Kind of quiet."

"Like how quiet?" Deja asks.

"I don't know. Just quiet."

Nikki can tell that Deja is disappointed. As a future writer, Nikki should have more details. But there just aren't any more.

"Can you draw a picture of him?"

"No, I can't draw a picture of him. You know I don't draw good."

"I wish I had seen him," Deja says. "I bet I could draw a picture of him. It's not fair that you got to see him and you can't even draw a picture of him."

"But you'll be able to see him at the wedding," Nikki reminds her.

Deja doesn't say anything. She's suddenly busy looking at her aunt's car in their driveway.

Nikki finds that strange. It's too early for Deja's aunt to be home. Usually Deja has to wait a while at Nikki's until her Auntie Dee gets home from work.

"See you later, Nikki," Deja says, turning up her walkway.

Nikki practically dances into her house. Her mother is on the telephone, and it's all she can do not to interrupt her—as she's been warned not to do so many times in the past. But her mother's conversation seems to go on and on and on. It's torture. Several times it really seems as if she's just about to get off the phone, but then she starts up again on a whole different topic. Finally Nikki places herself smack-dab in front of her mother, standing there very still but with a pained look on her face.

At last her mother says, "Flo, let me call you back. Nikki just got home, and I think she needs to tell me something."

As soon as the receiver is back in its charger, Nikki bursts out with, "Mommy, you're not going to *believe* what happened today!"

Her mother smiles. "What happened?" she asks.

"First, we all found out that Ms. Shelby is getting married in less than two weeks!"

"Oh, my, how wonderful," her mother says, sounding pleased.

"But that's not the best part," Nikki rushes on. "Look what I got." She rummages in her backpack. Tucked away in her math book—so it wouldn't get bent—is the beautiful white engraved invitation with all the personal information about her teacher's wedding. Nikki slips it out of the envelope, then runs her fingertips over the embossed letters. At the top of the invitation are the words: *Mr. and Mrs. Floyd Shelby request the honor of your presence . . .*

"Ms. Shelby's first name is Felicia, and her parents are Mr. and Mrs. Floyd Shelby!" Nikki exclaims.

"Well, you know she had to have a first name, and she had to have parents. But where did you get that invitation?"

"From Ms. Shelby!"

"Ms. Shelby gave you an invitation to her wedding?"

"Yes, Mom. . . . Ms. Shelby really wanted to invite her whole class, but she could only invite two students. So she had this drawing where she put everyone's name in an old tissue box. And then she took out two names—without looking. All fair and square. And she pulled out my name. And, guess what else!"

Nikki's mom looks like she's mentally running to catch up and take it all in. "What?" she asks.

"The other name she pulled was *Deja's!*"

"What? Oh, my."

"It was fair and square. Ms. Shelby said. It was all fair and square."

"I'm sure it was," Nikki's mom says slowly. "What a coincidence."

Nikki races on to other things. "Mom, I need to get a present for Ms. Shelby, and I need to get a new dress and new shoes, because my old ones pinch, and I need to get my hair done—"

"Wait. Hold on, Nikki. Let me see that invitation."

Nikki hands it over, and she and her mother stare down at it. The wedding is less than two weeks away. *Less than two weeks!*

3

Bad, Bad News
Deja

Deja runs up her porch steps. She's in a hurry to see why Auntie Dee is home so early. She finds her in the living room, just hanging up the telephone. Deja feels happy—happy and puzzled at the same time. At least she won't have to wait a long time to tell Auntie her good news.

The serious expression on Auntie's face worries Deja for some reason. And the way Auntie Dee carefully puts the receiver back onto the charger. She turns to look at Deja without speaking. Deja doesn't think she's going to like what Auntie has to say.

"Come here, Deja, and sit down."

Uh-oh, Deja thinks as she takes her place next to her aunt.

"I have bad news," Auntie Dee says.

Deja doesn't like her serious tone. She braces herself.

"There have been some layoffs at work."

This isn't sounding good.

"The theater company is struggling with raising money, so they've had to let some people go—just for a while," Auntie adds quickly.

Deja wonders if Auntie Dee is one of the "let go" people. She holds her breath.

"I'm afraid they've had to let me go." Auntie smiles slightly. "Just for a while. I'm sure I'll be back to work in no time."

Deja thinks about this. "Does that mean we won't have any money?" she asks carefully.

"We won't have as much," Auntie Dee says.

Deja thinks some more. Finally she asks, "Are we going to be homeless?" That last word is so scary. She's seen lots about homeless people on the news. Maybe they'll have to live in Auntie's car and wash their clothes in a gas station bathroom. Maybe Nikki's parents will let them live with them. Even that thought isn't very pleasant. Anyone would get tired of having extra people in the house after a while.

"No, sweetie," Auntie says, laughing. Deja feels a little better. "We're not going to be homeless."

Still, Deja wonders. How can Auntie really know that?

"We're just going to have to tighten our belts."

Immediately Deja thinks about what this could mean. She doesn't think it will allow for a new dress and new shoes and a wedding present. She doesn't think it will mean anything good. It could mean just eating out of their garden. Or maybe they'll only be able to eat the food that you dig out of a bin with a shovel at the health food store—like beans and yucky grains. No more good-tasting stuff that comes already measured and packaged.

That night, Deja goes to bed picturing Auntie sitting at one of those big looms, weaving cloth for their clothes. Deja is pretty sure "tightening our belts" is not going to be fun.

She's still pondering this over her oatmeal the next morning when Nikki knocks on the kitchen door. She's come by to walk with her to school. Auntie is in her office doing something on the computer. Deja feels she has to tell Nikki, who seems eager to get to school. Deja can tell this from the way Nikki's staring at every bite of oatmeal Deja puts in her mouth.

"Oh, I have something for you," Nikki says.

Deja looks up. "What?"

From her backpack, Nikki takes out a piece of folded paper. She unfolds it and places it on the table in front of Deja. "I tried to draw a picture of Ms. Shelby's fiancé. This is kind of what he looks like."

Deja looks at Nikki's drawing. Nikki's right. She really can't draw.

"Ooh, ooh . . ." Nikki continues. "Guess what? I get to buy a new dress and get my hair done, and on Saturday my mom and me are going to Rendells, where Ms. Shelby is registered—you know, where they have a list of what she wants for a wedding present—and then we're going to look at the list and get her something from it. Like a blender or a Crock-Pot or maybe a fancy vase. Something like that—"

Deja cuts her off by sighing loudly. "Do we all the time have to be talking about Ms. Shelby's wedding?"

Nikki looks a little hurt. "We haven't been all the time talking about it."

"Yes, we have. And I'm getting tired of it."

"What's wrong with you?" Nikki asks.

Deja shakes her head. "Nothing."

"Did you tell your aunt about Ms. Shelby?"

In a small voice Deja says, "Not yet."

"You didn't tell her about the drawing and how Ms. Shelby picked our names and how we get to go to her wedding? And how you get to take your auntie as a guest, and I get to take my mom?"

"Not yet," Deja says again.

"Why?"

"I just haven't told her yet."

Nikki looks at her closely. "What is it, Deja?"

"I don't know if I want to go."

"What?" Nikki exclaims, incredulous.

"Well, Auntie Dee might not be able to take me."

"Then you can go with my mom and me."

Deja sighs. She gets her backpack and heads for the door.

"Well, if you don't want to go, you *should* give someone else your invitation. Someone who'd probably be really happy to get it."

Deja says nothing. For a few moments they walk along silently. Then Deja can't take it anymore. She has to tell Nikki what's going on.

"I have bad, bad news, Nikki. Bad, bad news." She takes a deep breath. "I'm not going to be able to get a new dress, and I'm not going to be able to get Ms. Shelby a present, and I'm not going to be able to get my hair done. I'm not going to be able to get anything new for a long, long time because we're not going to have any money. Because my auntie doesn't have a job anymore!"

Nikki's mouth drops open. She looks almost frightened. "Really?" she gasps. Deja wonders if Nikki is already picturing her and Auntie Dee homeless and going to the food bank at that church on Marin.

"What is your auntie going to do, Deja?"

Deja shrugs. "I don't know." Then she adds, "But don't tell anybody."

The rest of the walk to school is quiet. It seems as if Nikki feels she needs to be careful, in light of this new situation. "Are you still going to live next door?" she asks as they go through the school gate.

"Yeah, I think so."

Nikki sighs with relief.

The second bell has already rung. Now kids are walking to their lines. Nikki and Deja find their places and wait for Ms. Shelby to come and get them.

"Look at this," Rosario says from behind Deja. She has drawn a picture of Ms. Shelby's fiancé.

Nikki looks at the picture and shakes her

head. "He doesn't look anything like that," Nikki says. "Not even a little bit."

Ms. Shelby has put "Open" on the board for their morning journal topic. Usually this presents a challenge to Deja. Nikki is the one who likes to write, not Deja. She pulls out her journal and stares at the cover, which she's decorated with big and little stars. She admires that for a bit, then opens it to the first clean page. Across the top she writes: "Bad Bad News."

Bad Bad News

I'm getting ready to have some hard hard times. My auntie Dee told me yesterday that we're going to have to tighten our belts, because she doesn't have her job anymore. At her work they ran out of money or a lot of people weren't donating enough money to the place where she works and they had to let some people go. This is strange because it makes it sound like people want to go and someone has to let them. But I know my auntie did not want to go. She loved her job because it was mostly fun and she got to meet a whole bunch of different people and she said it didn't even feel like work. That's why she's sad that she doesn't have it any more. So we're not going to be able to get goodies from the store or any new stuff and maybe we'll have to start taking the bus because of expensive gas and maybe we'll have to grow all our own food and make our own ice cream. And maybe I'll have to wear shoes even when they get too small and pinch. But I'm glad I have a house now and it's still warm and I have my own bed and my own desk and closet and I still have clothes hanging in my closet but I might have to wear them a long time even when they get too little. Maybe my auntie can learn to weave cloth and sew that cloth and make me new clothes and

Deja isn't finished when Ms. Shelby tells them to put their journals away and get out their Sustained Silent Reading books while she takes attendance. But Deja does what she says. Then Ms. Shelby proclaims, "I need the office monitor to take the attendance and lunch count to the office." Deja looks up to see Nikki with the special folder. Maybe she'll see Ms. Shelby's fiancé again. Nikki has all the luck.

The Wedding Planners Club
Nikki

Rosario has started a club. It's called the Wedding Planners Club. At recess she explains that there is really such a thing as a wedding planner. It's a real job. In fact, she's probably going to be a wedding planner when she grows up.

"Me, too," Ayanna says. "That's what I'm going to be when I grow up."

"Me, too," ChiChi says, and soon nearly everyone has decided that they are going to be wedding planners as well. Rosario decides that those who want to be in the club have to plan Ms. Shelby's wedding—*everything* about it. She looks around to see if this discourages anyone. But Ayanna seconds the idea, and everyone's attention is completely focused on Rosario as she spells out what they'll be doing: designing the dresses for Ms. Shelby and her bridesmaids, planning the menu, choosing the decorations (flower arrangements and silverware settings and stuff that goes on the tables), writing the invitations, and more.

"This way," Rosario explains, "it'll be like we get to go to the wedding, too."

"I'm doing another cake," Keisha says. "A better one."

There's a chorus of "Me, too."

"We should have a wedding planner contest," Rosario says. "We should break into teams and plan Ms. Shelby's wedding with pictures and stuff. Then we can get some girls from the other third grades to vote for the best one. On Friday. That gives us two days." Rosario looks around as all the girls enthusiastically nod their heads.

For the rest of the day—during math, during social studies, during language arts, and even during P.E.—Nikki hears the words *flowers, menu,* and *color scheme* whispered. She even hears the word *registry.* Nikki has told the girls all about the registry, launching fresh excitement. Nikki thinks that's the part about weddings and wedding planning they all must like the best: picking out the stuff they would want people to give them. Several times when the class is supposed to be studying multiplication facts for the quiz on Friday, Ms. Shelby has to remind them that this quiet time is study time. She shouldn't hear any talking.

During SSR, Nikki passes a note to Deja just as Ms. Shelby turns from the board to look over the class. Deja quickly stuffs the note in her desk. As Ms. Shelby flips through her giant teacher's edition for more problems to write on the board, Deja carefully brings out the note and reads it quickly. Nikki has written:

When I get home I'm going to look in my mother's catalogs for some really good presents.

When Deja looks over at her, she seems miserable. Nikki instantly feels guilty. She'd forgotten all about Deja's very bad news. She hopes Deja doesn't think that she doesn't care. Because she does—when she remembers to.

Ms. Shelby gives those who have finished all their work—and those whose cards are still green (the good color on the behavior chart)— ten minutes of free time at the end of the day. They can spend it on a class project or at the jigsaw puzzle table or reading. Rosario must have met all the criteria because at 2:50 exactly, she says, "Ms. Shelby, ChiChi, Keisha, and me have all our work done and our cards are still green. Can we work on this special project we have?"

Ms. Shelby is sitting at the kidney-shaped table with some kids who are having a hard time with two-place multipliers. She looks up. "Okay, but make sure you use your indoor voices," she says, sounding distracted.

ChiChi, Keisha, and Rosario hurry to the class conference table, which is long and rectangular and is located next to the class library, in the corner. Nikki glances over at them. She's bubbling with excitement. She doesn't want to be left out. She starts to work really fast on her math problems, hoping she isn't making a lot of careless mistakes. Ms. Shelby says it's easy to make careless mistakes in math if you rush. She glances over to see Deja looking like she's taking her time.

At last, Nikki finishes her work and jumps up from her chair to march her math paper to Ms. Shelby's in-basket. As soon as she returns to her seat, her hand flies up. She doesn't even wait to be recognized. She just blurts out, "Ms. Shelby, can I have free time, too? My color's still green and I finished all my work."

Ms. Shelby sighs. *She's probably getting tired*

of all the interruptions, Nikki thinks. Over the next five minutes, Ms. Shelby is interrupted five more times as the girls in the Wedding Planners Club ask for free time to go to the class conference table.

Nikki loves the conference table. It's their class art center, so it's already equipped with colored pencils and markers and scissors and big sheets of construction paper in a neat stack. There are still some splatters of dry paint on it, from when the class made papier-mâché globes for social studies. Nikki loves the feeling of independence she has whenever she goes to it. It's a busy table, even when no one is working there. Each girl approaches it with an excited look on her face.

Nikki wonders what's taking Deja so long. Finally she sees her take her paper up to the classwork basket and then, on her way back to her desk, stop by the kidney-shaped table to ask quietly if she can join the other girls. Ms. Shelby nods without looking up from helping Ralph.

Lost cause, Nikki thinks, glancing back at Ralph.

Rosario has decided that they should form their teams now. As soon as she gets the words out of her mouth, nearly everyone at the table starts whispering frantically about who they want on their team.

"We have to do it organized," Rosario says.

"But there's only seven of us," ChiChi observes.

Then a startling thing happens. Antonia, Deja's nemesis, puts her math paper in the in-basket, gets Ms. Shelby's permission, and saunters over to the conference table. She takes a seat and folds her hands as if she's waiting for something. "I'd like to be a wedding planner, too," she says calmly.

Everyone looks at one another. Then Rosario speaks up. "Okay."

"Good. Now we have an even number," ChiChi adds.

Rosario empties the marker box and says, "Let's write our names on pieces of paper, fold them up real good, and I'll pick out two names for team captains. And then they get to pick who they want on their team."

Rosario looks over her shoulder at Ms. Shelby, takes a piece of construction paper, and folds it in half three times. She tears it along the folds and hands everyone a piece.

Each girl writes her name on her paper, folds it up carefully, and drops it into the empty

marker box. Rosario, continuing to run the show, pulls out the first piece. "Keisha," she says as soon as she unfolds it. She pulls out a second paper. "Antonia," she says. Nikki sees Deja frown. It's been a while since Deja and Antonia have clashed. It's almost as if they've called a truce.

"I should go first because my name begins with an *A*," Antonia says quietly.

Rosario agrees. "Okay, choose."

"Nikki," Antonia says.

Nikki can't believe her ears. "Me?" she asks.

"Yes, you," Antonia says.

Nikki looks at Deja, but Deja just gives her a little shrug. Nikki frowns. *Why is Deja acting like that?* she wonders.

Once the teams are made—Antonia, Nikki, ChiChi, and Ayanna on one team, and Keisha, Deja, Rosario, and Yolanda on the other—they decide to name them.

"We're going to call our team the Pink Roses," Antonia says.

"I don't want Pink Roses," Nikki objects. "I want Red Roses."

"Raise your hand if you want Red Roses," Antonia says. The hands of all her teammates go up. Antonia rolls her eyes and crosses her arms. "Okay, we're the Red Roses."

"I want the Purple Lilacs," Deja says quickly.

"I want yellow lilacs," Keisha insists.

"Hah, hah, hah. There's no such thing," Deja says with certainty.

Nikki wonders if there are yellow lilacs.

"Orange, then."

"There's no orange lilacs, either," Deja proclaims, and then adds quickly, "All those for Purple Lilacs, raise your hand."

Slowly, everyone on the team raises her hand.

So it is the Purple Lilacs against the Red Roses.

Rosario has something more to say. "Let's do four things: wedding and bridesmaid dresses—and no tracing from a book; wedding menu—and it has to be from real recipes, like from real cookbooks; decorations like the tables and that altar thing; and the invitation—on really nice paper, not on notebook paper." She looks around.

"What about the registry?" whines Yolanda.

"No. We don't have time for all that," Rosario says. "How many want to do a registry?" she adds, probably to seem fair.

Three hands go up: Keisha, ChiChi, and Yolanda.

"No registry," Rosario says.

Then Nikki, ChiChi, Ayanna, and . . . *Antonia* scoot their chairs down to the end of the rectangular table and put their heads together. Nikki wonders how Deja feels, seeing Nikki putting her head together with Antonia's. One thing's for sure: Deja is probably going to try to take over organizing her group.

Antonia says, "I think we should divide everything up—the jobs and stuff."

"I want to do the dress. Something better than that stuff we already did before we were competing against each other," ChiChi says.

"I want to do the decorating," Antonia says quickly, before anyone else can claim the task. "That's the flowers and the tables and all that stuff. And party favors," she adds.

"I don't know if weddings have party favors," Nikki says.

"I think this wedding should. People like to take stuff home," Antonia insists, and no one challenges her.

"My aunt took the centerpiece home from her friend's wedding," ChiChi says.

Everyone looks at ChiChi with interest.

"I want to do the menu," Nikki jumps in, before someone else claims it. She'd just overheard Deja stating to her team that she wanted to do the menu. It will be fun for them both to do it.

"Then I guess I'm doing the wedding invitation," Ayanna says.

On the way home, Nikki is lost in thought about the menu. Deja doesn't have much to say, either. Then Nikki remembers Saturday and how that's the day she'll get to go shopping. She already knows that she wants to get a dress in peach or lavender. She just needs to decide which color. She poses this dilemma to Deja.

"I know you'll probably say I shouldn't get the lavender one, since that's your favorite color, but what I want to do is try them both on—that is, if they're in my size—and see which one looks better on me." She stops for a breath then asks, "What do you think, Deja?"

"Fine," Deja says.

It doesn't sound very fine to Nikki, though. She looks over at Deja. "But what do you think?"

"Whichever one looks the best," Deja says quietly.

"Yeah, that's what I think," Nikki agrees. She sneaks a look at Deja again. Deja looks sad, and for a few seconds Nikki feels guilty about her own excitement.

There's a moment of silence, then Nikki pipes up with, "Ooh, Deja, ask your auntie if you can come with us on Saturday. It'll be so much fun if you can come with me."

"Oh, yeah, sure," Deja says.

"Isn't it great that we're both doing the menu for our teams?" Nikki goes on, since Deja is being so glum and quiet. "I can't wait. I'm going to do something different. I've got ideas!"

They reach Deja's driveway, where Nikki sees Deja's auntie's car. She feels a little bad about Deja's aunt, but she can't linger on that. She's got things to do—really important things.

Nikki starts for her own house. "See ya, Deja. Don't forget to ask your auntie about Saturday."

5

All Figured Out
Deja

Deja takes a deep breath before she pulls out the key on its string around her neck and unlocks the front door. She needs to tell Auntie about the wedding before she asks if she can go with Nikki on Saturday.

Auntie is in the kitchen. Deja puts her backpack on the stairs. Dragging her feet, she walks through the kitchen door.

"Hi, sweetie," Auntie Dee says, looking up. She's stirring something in a big mixing bowl with a wooden spoon.

"Hi, Auntie Dee." Deja looks into the bowl, hoping for cake batter. It's batter all right, but there's something shredded and green in it.

"Zucchini bread," Auntie says happily. "I found the recipe in the newspaper."

Deja watches the spoon go around and around. "Oh," she says.

"What's wrong, honey?" Auntie asks. It's as if she's just then noticed Deja's downturned mouth and slumped shoulders.

Deja decides to dive in. "Ms. Shelby is getting married. Saturday after next."

Auntie Dee stops stirring and puts both palms on the counter. "Oh, my!"

"She really wanted all her students to go to the wedding, but she didn't have enough room for everybody to come."

"Well, of course not," Auntie says.

"But she was able to invite two."

Auntie Dee brightens.

"One of those persons was Nikki."

"Wow," Auntie says happily, then quickly adds, "Oh, honey, I hope you're not too disappointed that it wasn't you."

"I got one, too," Deja says.

Auntie's smiling demeanor immediately returns. "Oh, Deja! How wonderful!"

"But I don't want to go."

Auntie Dee looks puzzled. "Why?"

Deja can't hold back her fears any longer. "Because we're not going to have any money. For a present from this special registry that Ms. Shelby has at Rendells or for a new dress for me,

or for new shoes, or—for anything! And I'm not going to be able to get my hair done."

Auntie moves to the table and sits down.

Deja takes the chair across from her. She feels better, for some reason. As if her auntie is just getting ready to tackle the problem.

"Listen," Auntie Dee says, sounding certain. "We're going to solve this thing. I know we are. You just leave it to me."

Deja gets her backpack and pulls out the invitation. She opens it and shows Auntie one of the little cards that's inside the envelope. "Look at this little card where you can choose what you want to eat."

Auntie takes the invitation out of her hand. "Oh, look, you can bring a guest—which of course will be me." She points out the place where it says "Invitee plus guest." She smiles as if she's got it all worked out, as if she knows just how she'll come up with enough money for new clothes, a present, and a beauty shop visit for Deja.

Later, when Deja is doing her homework at the kitchen table, Auntie Dee calls to her from the living room. As soon as Deja appears, Auntie pats the place beside her on the couch. Deja sits down and waits.

"Now listen," Auntie says. "I was just on the phone with Miss Ida. I told her all about you being invited to your teacher's wedding and all about our circumstances, and guess what she said."

Deja shrugs. Whatever is coming, she knows it's not going to be all that great. Auntie Dee will think it's great, but Deja knows her feelings won't match her aunt's.

"Come to find out, Miss Ida was a seamstress in her day. She has offered to make you a new dress." Auntie beams as she waits for Deja's response. Her smile is extra wide, extra encouraging.

"Oh," Deja says. She thinks back on the time when she had to stay at Miss Ida's; the time when Auntie Dee had to go out of town. Everything in Miss Ida's house was old. Old curtains, old stove and refrigerator, an old television. It was awful staying there. At first. But then it got a little better. What kind of dress would Miss Ida come up with? Maybe something with a big bow in the back, like one of those dresses little girls wear on that show about pioneers—with big puffy sleeves.

"Auntie, I don't want to look like a pioneer girl."

Auntie laughs. "Don't worry, you won't. We'll

go to pick out the fabric and pattern on Saturday."

That makes Deja feel only a little bit better. Then she remembers the other problems. "But what about Ms. Shelby's present and my hair?"

"Don't worry about the gift. I have something very special for Ms. Shelby. And believe me, she won't be getting two of what we're going to give her."

"Are you going to tell me what it is?"

"Our kente cloth runner."

Deja looks over at their dining room table. Auntie Dee has always loved the long, colorful piece of cloth that decorates it. Auntie's best friend, Phoebe, brought it back for her all the way from Ghana, which is in West Africa. How will they be able to get another one?

"But you love that runner."

Auntie Dee shrugs. "Don't worry about that. Who knows? Maybe we'll go to Africa and get another one."

Deja thinks about that for a minute. Is she joking? Africa is so far away.

Auntie goes on, "And Phoebe is going to do your hair."

Deja frowns, and her auntie holds up her hand. "Don't jump the gun. She's going to do a great job."

But Deja doesn't want to give Auntie's best friend, Phoebe, a chance. She doesn't want to give Miss Ida a chance, either. And the thought of Auntie Dee giving up her beloved kente cloth—that just makes her feel worse.

"Have I ever led you wrong?" Auntie asks with a twinkle in her eye.

"No," Deja admits, and it's true. Auntie has always come through for her.

6

Big Plans
Nikki

Nikki is in the kitchen poring over a cook-book. She's just come across a beautiful picture of little cakes the size of ring boxes—called *petit fours*—when Deja knocks on the door. Nikki quickly puts a folded napkin on the page before she closes the book. Then she opens the door.

Deja is standing there with her backpack. "Wanna do homework together?" she asks.

"I guess," Nikki says, even though she's not very happy about the interruption. She'd really like to get back to looking at the petit fours recipe. Petit fours are going to be her secret weapon, but she has only a little bit of time to work on it.

Nikki's plan is to present a tasty sample of the

dessert she's going to include on her menu to each of the girls who'll be judging the wedding planners teams. She can't let Deja know about this plan because Deja would just copy it.

Deja seats herself at the table. She glances at the cookbook. But then she seems to turn her attention to emptying stuff from her book bag. She takes out her spelling folder and her pencil and her pencil sharpener. Nikki knows that Deja hates a dull pencil. Deja reaches for a napkin, places it on the table before her, and carefully sharpens her pencil over it. When she looks up, she says, "What's wrong?"

"What do you mean?" Nikki asks.

"Why are you sitting there looking at me? Where's your homework?"

"Oh, yeah." Nikki gets up and retrieves her backpack from just inside the front door. As soon as she returns, she sees the cookbook in front of Deja, opened to the page with the petit fours recipe.

"What's this?" Deja asks.

"My mom's cookbook."

"What were you doing with it?"

"Nothing—just looking at it."

Deja looks at the beautiful picture of pastel-colored petit fours decoratively placed on a crystal cake plate. "Why were you looking at this page?"

"I was looking at the whole book, not just that page."

Deja stares at Nikki. Nikki can feel Deja's eyes on her even as she starts pulling stuff out of her backpack. It's quiet except for the ticking of the rooster clock on the wall.

"You're going to make something from your mom's cookbook, aren't you? Then you're going to bring it to school so you won't just have a menu, you'll have real food, too," Deja says. "Admit it, Nikki."

"It's my idea, and you can't copy, otherwise you're a copycat."

"I'm not copying your stupid idea. Anyway, your mom is not going to let you do it. You're too young to cook."

"My mom will let me do it. She let me help make those election day cookies when you were running for student body president of Carver Elementary School."

"Those cookies were already made. We just had to put them on a cookie sheet and put them in the oven. You can't just make something from scratch."

"Oh, yes, I can."

"No, you can't."

"Yes, I can," Nikki persists.

"Did you get permission?"

"Not yet, but I'm going to."

Deja chuckles. "Here," she says, handing Nikki the list of that week's spelling words. "Test me."

After Deja goes home, Nikki begins to worry. Deja might just steal her idea. She could get her auntie to make something yummy for the judges—and then Deja's team could win the contest. Nikki decides to get back to her spelling words later. She has petit fours to make.

But first she has to get some kind of permission. That's going to be tricky. Only her father is home. He's in the den watching football and he's not going to want to be disturbed. Nikki knows it must be a close game, because her father has been doing a bunch of whooping and hollering and talking bad about one of the teams. Perhaps this can work in her favor.

She walks quietly to the den doorway and looks in. Her father is sitting on the edge of his special recliner with his eyes glued to the TV screen. Suddenly he jumps up, throws his fist in the air, and does a little dance in place. Nikki sighs. She has to see or hear this scene almost every week.

His huge grin tells her that this is a perfect

time to ask him for permission. He won't even register what she's asking. She could probably ask him for permission to drive the car and he would say yes.

"Daddy?" she says in her sweetest voice.

"Yeah, baby, what is it?"

Good sign, Nikki thinks. "Can I . . . make some petit fours?"

"What?" His total attention is on the replay.

"Some petit fours."

"Petit fours—what are those?"

She knows he's still not really paying attention.

"These little cakes."

He stops then and looks at her squarely. "Have you made those before?"

"No," she says truthfully. "But I looked in the recipe book and they're really easy to make."

If a touchdown hadn't been scored just then, her father might have asked her more questions. But now he's so excited about the game, all he can do is make a brushing-away movement with his hand and yell out, "Yeah, sure!" Then he adds, "Be careful."

Good. She has the permission she needs. Now the trick is to get everything done before her mother gets home from her book club meeting.

Nikki has watched her mother in the kitchen enough to know that she needs to get out all the ingredients and utensils and line them up on the table. She knows how to measure, pretty much, and she knows the different cups for dry ingredients and liquid ingredients. But she doesn't know stuff like "sift dry ingredients." And what's a *level* tablespoon? And how do you soften butter? And then there's the eggs. What does it mean to separate them? And what's *confectioners'* sugar? Maybe it's just another way of saying sugar. And what's *corn* syrup? Do they have any? Maybe she can use maple syrup or molasses.

First, she has to get out the regular sugar and measure a cup and a half. The canister is half full. Nikki wonders how she can get the sugar out of it and into the cup. Some will probably spill. She knows what she'll do. She puts the cup in the kitchen sink and pours the sugar into it that way. Unfortunately, she turns the canister over too far and the sugar not only fills the cup, but the remainder goes into the sink.

Oh, well, Nikki thinks. At least the mess can be rinsed down the drain.

Nikki studies the recipe again. She jumps up and preheats the oven to 350 degrees. She knows how to do that. Then she begins to measure and dump the rest of the ingredients into the big bowl her mother always uses. She doesn't pay any attention to the sifting part. *As long as everything is in the bowl,* she thinks.

She doesn't know what creaming butter and sugar together means, so she just puts those ingredients into the bowl as well. The eggs are in there, too—unseparated, because she doesn't know what that means, either. She grabs a big wooden spoon from the counter and begins to stir, but the stick of butter is not mixing in the way it should. The ingredients aren't turning into a batter, not like when her mother makes a cake. Nikki wonders if heating everything in the oven would help. That way, the butter will melt and she can stir everything together.

Nikki knows that you can't put a mixing bowl in the oven, so she dumps everything into a big roasting pan, mentally patting herself on the back for thinking of that. Then she watches it through the glass window in the oven door. When the butter is melted, she puts on her mother's big oven mitts and very carefully takes the roasting pan out. She places it on top of the stove and stirs everything together. It still doesn't really look like batter, but it's closer. She leaves it on the stove to cool while she figures out how to grease and flour a cake pan.

She has the pan. It's shaped like a rectangle

and is not too deep. But it's not greased and floured. While Nikki is looking for something to grease the pan with, she comes across the cans of frosting her mother keeps on hand. There's chocolate and vanilla. She decides to use it to decorate her petit fours. But she's also going to put strawberry jam on some of them so they will look more colorful.

When she feels the roasting pan is cool enough, she carries it—wearing the oven mitts—to the table and pours the batter into the cake pan. Then she puts the cake pan into the oven, happy that nothing got on the floor.

Oops . . . she realizes that she forgot to grease and flour the pan. *Oh, well,* she thinks. She's sure everything will turn out all right anyway.

Nikki knows to set the timer on the stove. She knows how to clean up after herself as well. Once she's finished, she opens the window to air out the kitchen and checks the wall clock. Her mother is due home in about an hour. Perfect. Her petit fours will be baked by then. The pan will be covered with foil and hidden under her bed, along with the cans of frosting and the jar of strawberry jam, and she'll be sitting at the table, putting her spelling words into a story and re-membering to underline each one.

✳

That's exactly how it works out. When her mom comes home, she sniffs the air in the kitchen suspiciously, but Nikki has done such a good job of cleaning up and putting things away that she doesn't ask any questions.

The next morning when Nikki wakes up and checks the cake under her bed, though, it has sunk in the middle. When she presses on it the way she has seen her mother do, it doesn't give. It's rock hard. *That's okay,* Nikki thinks. She gets out the knife she squirreled away in her dresser drawer and smears chocolate frosting on one part, vanilla frosting on another part, and strawberry jam on what's left. Then she saws the whole thing into squares. Well, they aren't perfect squares. They don't look anything like the pretty little pastel-colored petit fours pictured in her mother's cookbook.

Doesn't matter, Nikki tells herself. She manages to get most of her little cakes out of the pan and into the plastic container she had also sneaked into her room the night before. The container will go into her backpack, and no one will be the wiser—until lunch recess, when she surprises everyone with their own delicious little petit fours. It's all planned.

"What's that bulging out in your backpack?" Deja asks as soon as she sees Nikki come down her front steps.

"What?" Nikki asks.

"You've got something in your backpack."

"No, I don't."

"Nikki, anyone can see you've got something big and square in your backpack."

"Maybe, maybe not."

"Whatever," Deja says.

Nikki changes the subject. "What color do you like best on me, Deja? Peach or lavender?"

Deja looks over at Nikki suspiciously. "Here we go again. You know lavender is my favorite color."

"I like it, too." She glances quickly at Deja, then looks straight ahead. "You can't own a color, Deja."

"But *I* was hoping to wear lavender, Nikki."

"I thought your auntie couldn't get you anything new."

"She can't buy a dress already made from the department store. But she can get Miss Ida to make me something. We're going to look for a pattern and material on Saturday."

"You're not coming with me on Saturday?"

"I can't come with you and go with Auntie Dee at the same time."

Nikki looks disappointed. She was looking forward to having Deja as an audience: to watch her as she got her new dress and new shoes and bought a present from Ms. Shelby's actual registry.

"I know what you have in that stupid backpack, anyway," Deja adds.

Nikki is silent.

"It's something you made for the wedding menu. You think it's going to make your team win."

"I don't *think*. I *know*," Nikki says.

Deja rolls her eyes to show she doesn't care. Nikki knows better. And she knows that Deja probably didn't put all that much work into her menu, anyway. She probably just found some dishes out of Auntie's vegetarian cookbook. Yucky tofu and maybe nuts and dried fruit for dessert. There's no way Deja could help her team win with that stuff. Plus, a person can't own a color. Nikki is perfectly within her rights to choose a dress in lavender. Then a funny feeling comes over her. She spent so much time on the petit fours that she didn't put much time into her menu, either. None of the dishes even came out of a cookbook. Oh, well . . .

7

Roses vs. Lilacs
Deja

As soon as they enter the schoolyard, Rosario runs up to them. "Today's the contest, remember?"

"We remember," Deja says as unenthusiastically as possible.

"What's in your backpack?" Rosario asks Nikki.

"It's a surprise," Nikki says.

"It's something to go with her wedding menu," Deja says, not caring that she's spoiling the surprise.

Nikki sighs.

Rosario looks extra excited at this. She spreads the news once the bell sends them to Room Ten's lineup area. "Nikki brought something from her wedding menu!"

Deja is getting super tired of the word *wed-*

ding. She can't wait until the contest is over and they don't have to focus on Ms. Shelby's wedding anymore.

As soon as Deja puts her jacket in her cubby and takes her place at her desk, she's happy to see the morning journal topic: *What Really Bugs Me.*

She rummages around in her desk until she finds her morning journal. She loves opening to the first clean page when she has a lot to get off her chest.

Things Nikki is Doing to Bug Me on Purpose

My friend Nikki is really bugging me these days. And I know she's doing it all on purpose just because she gets to get a new dress and Ms. Shelby's present and new shoes and plus she gets to go to a beauty salon and get her hair done. And now we have this contest. A wedding planner contest where we all get to be wedding planners and ChiChi and Keisha and a bunch of other people know they want to be wedding planners when they grow up. And Nikki she's all the time talking about what she's going to do for the menu and the color of her dress and getting to see the registry for Ms. Shelbys present. She acts like she doesn't even care that I can't do those things. She's acting like everything is fine with me. I would be nicer to her if it was me that could do all those things and she couldn't. Now I wonder if she's a true friend. I just wonder.

She added that last part for emphasis. It makes her feel better.

Just as she's putting her journal away, a note is passed back to her. It's from Queen Rosario. (That's what Deja has come to call her, secretly.) The note reads:

> Isamar, Angela, Cynthia, and Myrella are going to be the judges. Bring everything you have to lunch recess.

Deja pulls her backpack off the back of her chair. She gets to keep hers with her because she isn't one of the kids who go into their backpacks all day looking for little toys or candy to sneak into their mouths. Like Ralph—he has to keep his in his cubby. Deja looks over at him, and sure enough, he's got some little action figure on his lap and all his attention is on it. Poor Ralph. He has such a hard time sticking to the rules.

Deja rummages around until she finds her menu. She looks it over:

WEDDING MENU

Beverages

Apple Juice
Water
Lemonaid
Rootbeer

Main Course

Tofu Spaghetti
Whole Wheat Bread
Spinach/Arugula Salad

Dessert

Soycream with Carob Sauce

Deja thinks it looks pretty good. She wrote it on a piece of folded lavender construction paper so it would look like a menu. And she decorated it with her usual rainbows and balloons. The only problem is the food itself—but Auntie only has vegetarian cookbooks. So what is she to do?

Just as she looks up, another note comes her way. It's from the queen once again:

> Its going to be 10 points for each thing so the team who gets the most points wins.

The Purple Lilacs and the Red Roses convene at an empty lunch table as soon as the bell rings, sending everyone to the yard for recess. Rosario—who thinks of everything, it seems—has already gotten permission from the teacher on lunch duty to use one of the tables.

"Roses over here," she says, indicating one end of the table. "And Lilacs over there." She indicates the other end. The judges are already there, standing with their arms crossed for some reason, probably trying to look serious.

Nikki has brought her mysteriously lumpy backpack with her.

Rosario goes on. "We're going to do wedding dresses and bridesmaids' dresses first, then the decorations, and then the invitation, and then the menu."

There are some blank looks; some shrugs. Without any more pomp and circumstance, Myrella picks up the Lilacs' poster board with a drawing of a bride in the middle. The bride looks as if she's wearing a fluffy white cloud on her head and a long, white gown. Deja can tell immediately that it was drawn by Rosario's older sister, the one in high school. She's seen Rosario's drawing and it's never been that good.

"Did you draw that?" Antonia asks.

"Yes," Rosario says.

"By yourself?"

"Yes, by myself."

"Let me see you draw it again," Antonia says.

"I don't have to, and anyway, we don't have time." Rosario turns to the judges. Angela has some index cards in her hand. "How many points do we get?" Rosario asks.

The judges put their heads together; then Angela writes a number on an index card and holds it up: 8.

Rosario grins. "Okay, hold up your drawing," she says to ChiChi of the Red Roses. ChiChi's is on two pieces of folded copy paper, one for the bride's dress, and one for the bridesmaids'. It looks as if she drew them while watching television. They're not very good.

"How many points?" Rosario asks eagerly.

The judges put their heads together again; then Angela holds up an index card with a four on it.

"Not fair," Ayanna protests.

"Is too," Rosario says.

"No, because ChiChi did hers and you didn't," Ayanna says.

"I did too do mine, and you can't prove I didn't."

That's the proof, Deja thinks. Rosario said, *You can't prove I didn't.* That's what guilty people always say.

"Let's do decorations next," Rosario says.

Antonia produces a thin three-ring binder. Her pictures are in plastic sleeves. "This is a picture of my table decorations," she says, holding up a drawing of four circular tables elaborately decorated with floral centerpieces and all the silver utensils and goblets and linen napkins depicted. There are little pouches of something above each plate. "These are my party favors. They contain gold foil chocolates in the shape of coins." She turns the page. There is a picture of an altar covered with flowers and doves. She moves it slowly before the judges as if she is reading them a picture book.

There is a collective "Wow!" Everyone is at a loss for words.

"Score?" Rosario asks, her voice flat and unenthusiastic.

The judges put their heads together. Then Angela holds up a ten. The Red Roses burst into loud whoops and clapping.

Deja sighs. It's already obvious which team will be called the best wedding planners.

Keisha, too, has a piece of copy paper from someone's printer, and all she has is a table depicted with plates and forks and knives and a vase of flowers in the middle. In the background is the altar with a few flowers drawn on—all daisies. *Anyone can draw a daisy,* Deja thinks.

Rosario, enthusiastic as ever, says, "Okay, what's the score?"

Angela holds up a card with a five on it.

The Red Roses are winning.

But then Yolanda comes through with the invitation. She must have copied a real one. The invitation is on cream-colored card stock, and she used a gold pen to write the words.

Angela, without being asked, holds up a card with a ten on it. The Purple Lilacs cheer and slap palms. They've just moved ahead. Ayanna's invitation earns only a four. She's made hers like an invitation to a kiddie birthday party, with lines for what, when, and where. It looks nothing like a wedding invitation.

Menus are next. "You go first, Deja," Nikki insists.

Deja knows it's because Nikki thinks hers is way better and she's going to win everyone over with her cake samples.

"What's tofu?" Ayanna asks as Deja's menu is passed around.

"It's stuff that's real healthy," Angela answers.

Deja takes her menu back and reads off

everything on it, from beverages to dessert, to a passive, perplexed audience. The judges already have their heads together, and when she finishes, they raise a card that has a seven on it. It's better than she expected. She shrugs and sits down.

Before Rosario can turn to Nikki, she has already unveiled her surprise samples and has begun passing out purple construction paper menus. There, in her mother's plastic Tupperware, are odd brown cubes that look like small wooden children's blocks. Some have clumps of chocolate frosting, some have vanilla, and some are smeared with red jam.

"First, I'll read my menu. Then each of you can have one of my petit fours, which is going to be my dessert."

The menus are written in marker. Nikki seems to be really proud of her creation. She reads to the group, "Appetizers (because you have to start with appetizers): Chocolate Chip Cookies or Corn Chips and Red Dip. Drinks: Lemonade or Root Beer or Coffee (for people who like coffee). Main Dish: Spaghetti or Fried Chicken and Potato Salad. Dessert: Petit Fours."

"Where's something green?" Deja asks. "You always have to have something green."

"No, you don't," Nikki says, looking annoyed.

"Your menu doesn't sound like something

from a cookbook. It sounds like you just thought it up."

"You can find all my dishes in any cookbook," Nikki says to Deja. Then she turns to the group. "I've brought samples of my petit fours. You all get to have one."

Nikki proudly holds out her plastic container to each girl so she can select one of her creations. A few look a little doubtful as they decide which to choose. Ayanna, perhaps in support of a team member, attempts to bite down on hers right away. ChiChi follows suit, but Antonia just looks at hers.

The Lilacs, with their petit fours in hand, wait and watch. As soon as they see Ayanna struggling to bite her little cake with her front teeth and switching to her side teeth, they try to bite down on theirs.

"This is like a brick!" Keisha says.

"I can't even eat mine!" Rosario seconds. "I can't even bite it. I could break my tooth!"

Deja doesn't say anything. She just tries real hard not to burst into laughter. She puts hers back in the container. As everyone protests that Nikki's dessert could break a tooth, the judges each grab a cake and attempt a bite, just so they can join in.

"This is worth a two!" Angela exclaims, not

bothering to hold up a card and not taking into consideration that the dessert represents only a part of the menu.

No one but Deja seems to notice the look on Nikki's face. When she snaps the lid onto the container and marches off, they all look after her, surprised. She doesn't even stop when the freeze bell rings. Rosario watches Nikki for a second, then announces, "We win! The Purple Lilacs are wedding planning champs!"

8

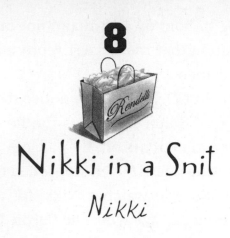

Nikki in a Snit
Nikki

Nikki knows she's lucky that she doesn't get into trouble. Mrs. Butler, the yard lady, is busy fussing at one of the big boys from fifth grade. She misses Nikki stomping across the yard to Room Ten's line. Nikki has nothing to say when Deja joins the line. Nothing to say when Deja tells her that her team, the Purple Lilacs, won the wedding planners contest. Nikki just gives one of those quick shoulder shrugs that a person can hardly see.

Nikki has nothing to say when Deja's auntie picks them up after school, either. Auntie Dee will get to pick them up all the time, now that she's not working. Both girls sit in the back seat, staring out of opposite windows.

"What's with you two?"Auntie Dee asks.

Nikki just shakes her head. She doesn't feel like talking. But then she thinks of what her mother would say about not answering an adult's question. "Nothing," she says.

"What do you have there in that plastic container?" Auntie Dee persists. The container sits primly on Nikki's lap.

Nikki looks down at it now. "Just something I made," she says in a very small voice.

Deja pipes up then. "Nikki made some little cakes to give out at our wedding planners contest."

Nikki looks over at Deja sharply, trying to decide whether Deja is making fun. She remembers the look on Deja's face and how she was trying not to laugh when everyone was talking bad about her petit fours. She didn't even try to stick up for Nikki. Plus, she put her own cake back in the container without even *trying* to eat it.

"Oh," Auntie Dee says cheerily, "I hope you saved one for me."

"There's a lot left over," Nikki says glumly.

"Yeah," Deja agrees. "There's a lot left over."

Nikki shoots Deja another look to check the expression on her face. But Deja looks perfectly innocent.

Nikki's mother is in the kitchen, frowning at the empty sugar canister in her hand. She looks up as Nikki puts her backpack on the table.

"Honey, your backpack doesn't belong on the table."

Nikki moves it to the bottom step of the stairs.

"Not there, either. Someone could trip over it. Put it on the floor next to the front door."

Nikki stomps back to the door and plops down the backpack heavily. When she returns to the kitchen, her mother is looking at her with a frown.

"Did someone have a bad day?"

Pouting, Nikki says, "No."

Her mother seems to ignore this. Instead, she asks, "What happened to the sugar? I'm sure I had enough left to make blueberry muffins, but . . ."

Nikki remembers the sugar she spilled in the

sink. "I don't know," she says, feeling her eyes grow big.

Her mother stares at her for a moment, then squints.

Nikki can't stay silent. "I tried to make some petit fours for my wedding planners team," she blurts out. Her eyes fill with tears.

"Your what?"

"We made up these wedding planners teams—just pretend—for Ms. Shelby's wedding. And I was the one who had to do the menu. What her guests would be eating and stuff. So I wanted to make a sample of my dessert. These petit fours I saw in your cookbook." Nikki is determined to rush through the next part of her explanation before her mother can fully understand that Nikki did something wrong. "So I got permission from Daddy—you were at your book club," she says to her mother's frowning face, "and Daddy said I could, but to be careful. And I was careful."

"But you used all the sugar. Why didn't you tell me?"

"I don't know," she says in a small voice, looking down.

"Never mind about that now. What's done is done. But no more making anything in this kitchen unless you get *my* permission."

Nikki nods and starts for the door, but her

mother stops her with, "Do you have any petit fours left?"

"I have a lot left."

"Well, let me see how they turned out."

Nikki gets her backpack and pulls out the plastic container. She'd planned to sneak the whole thing outside to the trash can, dump the cakes, wash the container in the bathroom, then sneak it back into the kitchen cabinet.

Now she opens the container and sets it on the table.

"My . . ." Her mother peers at the jumbled mound of hardened cubes. She plucks one out and attempts to bite down. "Whoa, that's pretty hard!" she exclaims, trying to chew. When she's finally able to swallow, she says, "Honey, next time let's do the baking together."

The rock cakes are forgotten the next morning when Nikki runs down the stairs. Saturday has finally come. She gets to go to the mall and look for a party dress and new shoes and a present for Ms. Shelby! Her feelings from yesterday have faded, but she's still mad at Deja for not coming to her defense when everyone was laughing at her. She thinks about how Deja has to go look for fabric and a pattern so Miss Ida can make her dress.

Nikki can't help smiling. She gets to buy something from Rendells. That gives her a special satisfaction. As Deja would say, "Hah, hah, and *hah!*"

The mall is full of shoppers. Nikki's mom has already decided where they will be going first. "We'll check the registry, and then we'll look for shoes and a dress for you."

That sentence alone fills Nikki's stomach with butterflies. It's so exciting to do all this shopping for herself and her teacher.

"Housewares with the bridal registry is on the third floor," her mother says, consulting the store map and then leading the way to the escalator. Nikki is always a bit careful about getting on escalators. They can be tricky. Before she can lose her nerve, her mother takes her by the hand and leads her on.

Housewares is full of . . . *housewares.* So much to choose from. Nikki's mom seems to be an old hand at registries. She knows just where to go. There's a kiosk next to the register that has a kind of computer attached. She pulls the invitation out of her purse, checks it, and then begins to type something on the screen. Before she knows it, Nikki sees a printer spit out a long white sheet.

You are here

"We'll go up to the café to look at it," Nikki's mom says, heading toward the escalators again. Nikki feels another flutter of excitement. While they sit in the café and pore over the list of possible wedding gifts, her mom drinks coffee and Nikki gets to drink hot chocolate. She thinks, *This is the most wonderful Saturday morning I've ever had.*

There are all kinds of things on the list: a queen jacquard embroidered comforter set in dusty green print; a plush gray towel set; a Bella Cucina juicer; special extra-firm pillows; a panini grill; a jumbo griddle; china settings (you can buy one place setting or more); a crystal goblet; a fancy silver fruit bowl; a special kind of spice rack; a collection of serveware; a silver frame; china vases . . . it all makes Nikki's head spin. She knows, more than anything, that she absolutely, absolutely, *absolutely* must have a big wedding when she grows up. She can't think of anything greater than giving her guests a long list of everything she wants. And them having to buy stuff from her list. What could be better?

They decide on the panini maker. "The next person who uses the registry will see that the panini maker is already bought," Nikki's mother explains. "That way your teacher won't get more than one." *This is marvelous,* Nikki thinks. *Everything about weddings is* wonderful!

After that, they head to the girls' department, then straight to the dressy dress section. Immediately Nikki sees the dress she wants. It has a wide satin sash and bodice and a chiffon skirt. It has little cap sleeves—which her mother likes—and comes in two colors: peach and lavender. In the dressing room, Nikki tries on the lavender first. Then she comes out so her mother can see it.

"It's perfect," her mother says. "That was easy. Take it off so we can buy it."

"I'm not getting it," Nikki says. She had made up her mind in the dressing room. "I'm going to get the peach one. Lavender is Deja's favorite color, and she can't get a new dress. Her aunt has to have one made for her. She'd only feel worse if I got the lavender one."

Nikki's mom looks surprised; then she smiles. "Good thinking," she says. And they're off to the shoe department.

"But I'm still mad at her," Nikki adds. She feels she has to get that in.

As they're heading for their car in the parking lot, Nikki holding the bag with her new shoes, and her mother holding the garment bag with the new dress in it and the bag with the panini grill, they run into Deja and her aunt heading to their car. Deja is holding a bag with LuAnn Fabrics written on it.

"Look who's here!" Nikki's mom says, smiling down at Deja. Nikki knows she's acting extra happy on purpose. Nikki's mom and Auntie Dee give each other a quick hug. *Why do women do that all the time,* Nikki wonders, *when they see each other unexpectedly?*

She, on the other hand, gives Deja as tiny a "hello" as possible.

Deja returns a tiny "hello"; then her eyes settle on the garment bag and quickly move to the bag in Nikki's hand. She looks down. While the grownups gush and talk about the usual things women talk about—Nikki isn't really listening—she and Deja just stand there, not speaking.

Finally Deja breaks the silence with "Are those your new shoes?" The question makes Nikki feel a little bit guilty.

"Yeah," she says.

Deja's eyes go to the garment bag again. But she doesn't need to ask, it seems. She says nothing.

After they part, each walking her own way, Nikki wishes she'd remembered to say to Deja about her new dress, "It's not *lavender!*"

9

Cool Days
Deja

On Tuesday morning Deja is sitting in the back of Auntie Dee's car, staring out of her window. Nikki is sitting beside her, but not very close. She's staring out of the opposite window, again. As usual, Nikki has almost nothing to say to Deja. Yesterday, Deja noticed that Nikki was sidling up to ChiChi at morning and lunch recess, and they'd gone off on their own to the jump rope area. In response, Deja purposely brought out her SSR book so she could read on the bench and not pay any attention to Nikki and her new friends. *Who cares?* Deja thinks. She isn't about to show that she notices that Nikki's been hanging around with someone else.

She thinks about Saturday morning at LuAnn Fabrics. Suddenly she feels a little scared. She and Auntie found a pattern for her dress for Ms. Shelby's wedding. They found beautiful satin and chiffon material. The word *chiffon* makes Deja think of pie heaped with whipped cream. There was lavender chiffon, and peach chiffon as well. Deja chose the peach because she suspected that Nikki had gotten her dress in lavender, even though she knew it was Deja's favorite color. Deja was determined not to be twins with Nikki.

"Not lavender?" Auntie had asked, holding up the lavender chiffon.

"No, I want the peach," Deja said.

She thinks about Miss Ida now, wondering if she'll really be able to follow the pattern's directions and make her dress look *exactly* like the picture on the front of the envelope. What if she can't? What if she makes it real sloppy and Deja has to wear it anyway?

At morning recess, Deja brings out her SSR book again and settles onto the bench to read it.

"What's wrong with you?"

Deja looks up, surprised to see Nikki standing before her.

"Nothing."

"Then why are you sitting over here by yourself?"

Deja supposes Nikki is just rubbing it in—that she has people to play with and Deja doesn't. "I feel like reading my book, that's all," Deja replies.

"Whatever," Nikki says, turning to get back to her friends in the jump rope area.

Deja sits there stewing. Nikki's probably happy that Auntie Dee lost her job. No, she probably doesn't even *remember* it. Hah, hah, and *hah,* that she got a two on her little cakes. Deja smiles, thinking back on it. She almost laughs.

At lunch recess, for the second day in a row, Nikki runs out ahead with Keisha and ChiChi to the jump rope area. Deja decides she'll jump rope, too. Why not? They don't own the jump rope area. Besides, she's good at jumping rope. She plans to jump and jump until the freeze bell rings. When Deja reaches them, they're already jumping double dutch: Nikki and Keisha are turning the ropes and ChiChi is jumping. Deja can't believe her eyes. Nikki, who has no rhythm, is turning the ropes—in rhythm! Who taught her that?

As if reading Deja's mind, Nikki says, "I can turn now. ChiChi showed me how."

"Well, la-di-da," Deja says, crossing her arms.

All three girls look over at Deja. Then Keisha and ChiChi look at Nikki, as if waiting to see how she's going to react to this.

Nikki, with ropes in hand, can only manage to roll her eyes.

Deja gets in the jump rope line. She'll show them.

"Regular," Deja says when it's her turn to jump.

Keisha and Nikki begin to turn with one rope. Deja steps back a few feet, then follows the rhythm of the rope with the palms of her hands until just the right moment. She jumps in and begins to chant: *"All last night and the night before, twenty-four robbers came knocking at the door. I got up to let them in, and this is what they said . . . One, two, three . . ."*

Deja is jumping with ease. She could do this all morning. When she gets to fifty-four, she feels the rope jerk beneath her foot, causing her to stumble.

"Out!" Nikki says. "Your turn, Ayanna!" Ayanna is next in line.

"I'm not out! You pulled the rope!"

"I did not!"

"You did, too!" Deja insists.

"Keisha, did I pull the rope?"

Keisha shrugs, as if she doesn't want to get in the middle of it.

"Out, Deja!" a girl from Mr. Miller's class yells. Then everyone in line begins to chant:

"You're out, Deja! You're out, Deja! You're out, Deja!"

Deja would like to punch that girl. She is not even in her room area. Room Sixteen has tetherball this week. She should tell Mrs. Butler on her. She should try to get that girl benched. Instead, Deja stomps off to Room Ten's lineup spot. She's tired of jumping, anyway.

The rest of the day pretty much follows the same pattern. Now Nikki is oh-so-tight with ChiChi and Keisha. Deja spies them passing notes to one another. At the end of the day, they use their free ten minutes to work on the class jigsaw puzzle together. It has five hundred pieces.

But Deja has an idea to get even. She'll invite Ayanna over to play Ping-Pong after school. Now that Auntie is home all the time, Deja can have company. With this in mind, she doesn't care a bit about the laughter coming from the puzzle table. She doesn't even care that Ms. Shelby has to tell them over and over to use their inside voices.

As soon as Ms. Shelby tells Deja's row to line up by the door to go home and is busy deciding which row is next, Deja turns to Ayanna behind her. "Can you come over? To play Ping-Pong?"

"I'll ask my mom," Ayanna says, looking a little surprised. "Can Rosario come?"

"I guess so," Deja says.

"And Suzanne from Mr. Beaumont's class? She lives on my block, and my mother gives her a ride."

"Okay," Deja says, a little unsure. Suddenly, she's not feeling so confident, but she can't back out now.

As she walks to Auntie's car, she thinks about how she'll go about getting permission to have company. She thinks about how Nikki will feel now that Deja has new and better friends.

"Where's Nikki?" Auntie Dee asks as Deja is fastening her seat belt.

"She's coming, I guess," Deja says. Once Ms. Shelby let everyone out of the class, Deja noticed Nikki lagging behind with Keisha and ChiChi. Deja thinks it's really rude for Nikki to keep Auntie Dee waiting. However, Auntie Dee must not think so, because she pulls a book out of her purse and starts to read. Auntie always carries a book with her just for times like this.

At last, Nikki strolls up and gets into the back seat. She greets Auntie Dee, then says to Deja, "I was with ChiChi and Keisha. They're coming over later."

"Well, Rosario and Ayanna and this girl from Mr. Beaumont's class are coming over to my house to play Ping-Pong." Deja quickly turns to Auntie Dee. "Is it okay?"

Auntie Dee puts her book away. "I suppose so." She looks back at Deja and then at Nikki. "What's going on?"

"Nothing," they both answer together. Any other time, they would have slapped palms for saying the same thing at the same time. Now they just stare straight ahead.

Nikki *and* Deja's guests arrive at almost the same time.

Deja takes Ayanna, Rosario, and Suzanne, the girl from Mr. Beaumont's class, outside to the Ping-Pong table. A rousing game begins, full of extra-loud laughter. Deja leads with the loudest laughter of all.

She wonders from time to time what Nikki is doing with *her* guests. She saw them from the kitchen window when they were dropped off together. She had gone inside to get drink boxes for everyone. Then Auntie brought out a tray of her healthy version of snacks: celery and bell pepper strips with peanut butter.

For a while, all is quiet on Nikki's side of the

fence. Deja looks up at Nikki's bedroom window at one point and sees that it is open. That encourages her to be even louder and to lead the other girls into being as loud as possible, too.

When she gets Ayanna out, she shouts, "You're out, Ayanna!" She practically leans her head back and aims this up at Nikki's window.

Rosario is the next to challenge her. Back and forth it goes until Deja sees her opening to slam the little white ball. Rosario misses. Deja leads loud cheers. Then Suzanne takes her place at the Ping-Pong table. She's good at the game. Back and forth the ball goes—on and on, while Ayanna and Rosario cheer first for Deja, then for Suzanne. On and on. . . . At one point, ChiChi comes to Nikki's window and looks down. She's soon joined by Keisha. Deja loves showing off. She sneaks a glance up at her audience. While she's busy doing that, Suzanne slams the ball hard, sending it quickly past Deja's attempt to return it.

"Out!" Rosario shouts.

It takes Deja a moment to realize she's really out. Then she hears laughter. It's coming from Nikki's window! Nikki is at the window with her guests. All three are pointing and laughing. *Extra loud,* Deja thinks. That's it, she decides.

She's never, *ever* going to be friends with Nikki again. *Never!*

A cool front moves in for the rest of the week. In the car going to and from school, Deja has nothing to say to Nikki, and Nikki seems to have nothing to say to Deja. And that's just fine. When Deja sees Nikki dash off at recess to join her new best friends, Keisha and ChiChi, she just joins *her* new best friends, Ayanna and Rosario. Deja likes it better this way, she tells herself. She'll just be friends with Ayanna and Rosario forever. And not miss Nikki even a little bit.

10

Wedding Day
Nikki & Deja

Nikki wakes very early on the *Big Day*. She looks at her dress hanging on the closet door. *So pretty,* she thinks. Her hair is in sponge rollers. She'd gotten it done after school the day before. After the beauty shop lady had finished, she'd looked in the mirror and thought that she could have been a movie star. Her hair looked so pretty. Last night she had to sleep in sponge rollers with a scarf tied over them so her hairdo wouldn't get messed up.

She looks at her new white patent leather shoes on the floor under her new dress. She has white tights to go with them, which are almost like stockings. She's going to look like a princess. She smiles thinking about this. Then she has a

vision of Deja in her homemade dress and laughs out loud. *Too bad I didn't get my dress in lavender,* Nikki thinks.

Deja had been so excited she could hardly fall asleep the night before. After they'd dropped Nikki off, she and Auntie Dee had gone directly to Miss Ida's and picked up Deja's dress for the wedding. Miss Ida brought it out in a plastic bag, just like the stuff you get at the cleaners. Deja had tried it on and then stood in front of Miss Ida's standing mirror in her bedroom. It was beautiful! Not homemade-looking or sloppy at all. She looked just like a princess. She loved her new dress, even if it was in peach instead of lavender. It went perfectly with her black patent leather shoes, which still fit. After that, they headed directly over to Auntie's friend Phoebe's so Deja could get her hair done.

Sitting in her bed now with sponge rollers in her hair, gazing at her beautiful peach princess dress hanging from the top of the closet door, Deja just knows she's going to look way better than Nikki. Hah, hah, and *hah!*

Nikki has no appetite. She's too excited. Her mother places a bowl of oatmeal in front of her, but she can eat only a few bites. She kind of wonders what Deja is doing right then.

It's all Deja can do to get down her cold cereal. It has those awful little flax seeds in it that she finds hard to eat. They keep getting stuck in her teeth. She wonders, just a little bit, what Nikki is doing right then. And she wonders what time Nikki and her mom are leaving for the wedding, which is at noon at a fancy hotel, followed by a fancy reception with lunch and cake. Deja is really only interested in the wedding cake. Oh, and she wishes she could see Ms. Shelby open all her presents. She looks over at the wrapped present she'll be bringing, sitting on the kitchen counter.

She thinks about the kente cloth table runner from Ghana. Will Ms. Shelby like it? One thing's for sure. She won't be getting another one like it. It came all the way from Africa.

The hotel has an atrium with tall palms that reach all the way to the ceiling. Deja looks up at the skylight and sees the clear blue sky. It is a perfect day for Ms. Shelby's wedding. Deja decides right then that she is going to have her wedding at the very same hotel.

Auntie checks the announcement board that

tells where all the events are. "Crystal Room," Auntie says, taking her hand and leading the way. Deja follows, feeling a surge of excitement for two reasons. She's going to see her teacher get married, and she just might run into her *best-friend-no-more*, Nikki.

A man in a uniform stands at the Crystal Room entrance. "Guest of the bride or groom?" he asks.

"Bride," Deja says happily. She loves saying the word, because *bride* means her beloved teacher, Ms. Shelby.

The uniformed man poses the same question to the people behind her.

"Bride," says a small voice that Deja recognizes. She turns around. It's Nikki. In a peach chiffon dress with a wide moss-green sash! Deja is stunned, but she hopes she's hiding it well.

Nikki is surprised as well. She knew she would see Deja eventually, but she didn't think it would be so soon, and not right in front of her. And she didn't think she'd see Deja in a peach-colored dress that looks almost like her own. Deja looks her up and down. "Hi," she says quietly.

"Hello," Nikki says, then looks away.

Auntie and Nikki's mom say hello and stand there scanning the seating. There aren't any rows with four seats together. An usher leads Auntie and Deja to two seats in the middle row, halfway up the aisle. Deja doesn't know where Nikki and her mom will be sitting. She doesn't dare look back.

The usher escorts Nikki and her mom to two seats five rows behind Deja and her aunt. When they sit, Nikki can no longer see Deja.

The music starts up, and everyone turns to see the groom and the groomsmen walk down the aisle. After they take their places on one side of the altar, Ms. Shelby's bridesmaids glide up the aisle and take their places on the other side of the altar.

Deja's mouth drops open. She wishes she could look back to see if she can find Nikki. She wonders what Nikki must think. Deja knows that she's probably never seen anything so beautiful.

Then the music changes to "Here Comes the Bride." Everyone stands and turns toward the entrance of the Crystal Room. Deja's heart begins to beat faster. Behind her, Nikki's heart begins to beat faster. Nikki's mom and Auntie Dee take out tissues from their purses. Slowly, Ms. Shelby, in the most beautiful white wedding dress Nikki and Deja have ever seen, begins her walk down the aisle on the arm of her father. Nikki and Deja both can't believe it. *Their teacher is getting married!*

The most exciting part happens after all the long, long stuff the man at the front says about marriage and vows and a bunch of other big words that Nikki and Deja don't even understand. It happens when that man gives the groom permission to kiss the bride.

Nikki holds her breath. Deja holds her breath. Their teacher's new husband leans over and kisses her . . . right on the cheek. Both girls clap their hands over their mouths to keep from bursting into laughter. Now Deja *really* wishes she could see Nikki's reaction. And Nikki wishes she could see Deja's face, too.

"He must be very shy," Nikki hears her mother say.

Nikki knew it! She could tell when she saw Ms. Shelby's fiancé in the office that time. She could tell he was the quiet, shy type.

Nikki and Deja watch their teacher go back down the aisle on the arm of her new husband, followed by the bridesmaids and groomsmen.

After a bit, everyone else gets to go down the aisle too, and out the double doors to the reception room next door.

There are so many people that the girls don't see each other. The room is filled with round tables with white tablecloths and silver place settings. Each table has a flower arrangement of white orchids and a card with a number on it at its center.

"Table twelve," Auntie says, looking around. "Help me look, Deja."

Deja looks around, but not for table twelve. She's trying to see where Nikki is.

At the same time, Nikki is searching the room for Deja.

"There it is," Nikki hears her mother say.

Auntie Dee finds their table just then as well.

Deja and Auntie Dee and Nikki and her mom arrive at table twelve at exactly the same time. There are four empty places, all together. When Auntie Dee and Deja's mom sit down, they leave the two seats between them empty. "Sit down," Auntie Dee says, before introducing herself and Deja to the other people at the table.

Nikki's mom tells her to be seated too, and then turns away to introduce herself to the elderly woman seated on the other side of her.

"Isn't this nice?" Auntie Dee says.

"It's absolutely lovely," Nikki's mom says.

Nikki and Deja don't say anything. A waiter comes by and places salad in front of them. Deja looks down at hers, then at all the silverware at her place setting. Nikki stares at her place setting as well.

"I've got too many forks," Deja says to herself.

"Me, too," Nikki mumbles. Her mother is busy talking to the elderly gentleman sitting two seats away. Nikki holds up the smallest one and studies it.

"I thought you were going to wear lavender," Deja says out of the blue.

"I decided not to," Nikki says. "Because lavender's *your* color."

"That's why you got your dress in peach?"

"Yeah." Nikki starts in on her salad with the little fork. "But why are *you* wearing peach?" she asks after a moment.

"'Cause I didn't want to be twins." Deja sneaks a look at Nikki to see how she takes this.

"And look," Nikki says, giggling. "We're twins anyway."

Deja can't help giggling, too. She takes a bite of salad, using the same size fork as Nikki.

Later, when the dessert cart comes around, they both choose strawberry shortcake.

After that, a cart comes around with gold boxes of wedding cake to take home.

"I'm keeping mine forever," Nikki says.

"Me, too," Deja says.

Then, in the middle of the reception, while everyone is eating the yummy desserts, music starts up. And there's their teacher, dancing with her new husband—something like a waltz. She still has on her flowing white wedding dress. Their teacher, dancing with her *husband* . . . Nikki and Deja look at each other and smile. They're speechless. This is just too amazing. Ms. Shelby is amazing, her dress is amazing, and the decorations are amazing, too. Watching their teacher dance with her new husband is amazing, and taking wedding cake home is *really* amazing. But the most amazing thing about all of it, both girls realize with surprise, is sharing this wonderful experience with each other.